THE LADY IN THE LAKE, THE LOCKED BOX, AND OTHER MYSTERIES

The Winter Winds Prevail

Kathy Lou Waskett

The Lady in the Lake

She was smiling. Her crystal blue eyes glistened as she met the maker of dreams and time. Her skin was taut and pale. Once red, her lips were now pale blue as the water surrounding her body.

In a nearby neighborhood, there was an older man whose life would change due to this incident.

Henry was looking out the window drinking his coffee. He told Marco, his dog, "The air is crisp and cold. I love to see the changes in the seasons. Think I'll take a walk and grab breakfast at the local diner."

Henry signaled for Marco to get in the backseat. Marco was happy to take a road trip. Henry drove to the lake and enjoyed looking at the trees covered with green, gold, and orange foliage. It was a beautiful autumn day, but few people were on the road this early. Henry parked his car by the lake and let Marco out.

Marco wagged his tail and started running towards the lake. Henry picked up a stick and walked towards the lake. Marco began to bark. His barking became more frequent as if he had discovered something.

"What did you find, Marco? A frog? A fish? Let me check it out!"

Henry March was not looking for anything in particular. However, curiosity got the best of him when he saw something in the reeds in the lake. He did not expect to see anything that would be significant. Then he thought, *Let me get a closer look. Nothing much happens at the lake.*

The object that Marco was barking at was a cold, lifeless form lying still near the coral and reeds. Henry's skin started to crawl, and his body shivered. Henry almost missed the female form, but his faithful dog,

Marco, found her body. Henry's collie mix started barking loudly and would not quiet down.

Henry stood there on the beach gazing intently at the young lady in the water. Henry did not know what to do. He pondered what his options were. Then he had a harrowing thought, *If someone brought her to the hospital, the doctors and nurses might think I had drowned this pretty lady.*

His fingerprints would be all over her if he rescued her. What a mess! "I can't just leave her there! Somebody must be looking for her," he muttered.

The lifeless form in the water seemed to draw him closer. It was as if the girl was crying for help. Henry started questioning himself. *Who was she? Why did this happen? Indeed someone is looking for her. I need to see if she is still alive and call the police!* he thought.

Without thinking, Henry walked out into the water, picked up the maiden's lifeless form, and laid her on the beach. First, he checked if she was still breathing and felt her pulse. Then, he got his cellphone out of his pocket and called 911.

"I found a body in the water of a young girl. I don't know how long she has been in the lake. She's still breathing but unconscious."

"We'll send someone right away, sir,: said dispatch.

As he ended the call, a sense of foreboding came upon him. The hairs on his neck stood up. Henry started getting nervous and muttered to himself, "I should have left the body alone and walked away!"

A luminous and eerie figure loomed in the distance. "The air sure feels cold and clammy this year. It must be my imagination. It must be just the shock of seeing the lady in the water. The police should be coming soon. No need to worry," Henry said. Then, he continued confidently, "Besides, I have my faithful dog to protect me. You've watched too many movies. It's morning, and there's no doom and gloom in the morning. Things happen at night."

Still, Henry was worried, and his heart filled with fear. Marco started barking and yelping in a panic. That was when he felt something hard hit his head, and the lights went out. Everything got dark.

Henry woke up in a hospital bed. He looked around and noticed that he was in a private room with cards and flowers on his nightstand. Then he started feeling an excruciating pain at the back of his head, and there was an IV hooked to his arm.

How did I get here? Where's my dog? Panicky thoughts raced through Henry's head. He tried to sit, but the pain from the blow to his head made him lie back down.

Fear took over, and his blood pressure shot up. The panicky thoughts continued to whirl in his mind. *What happened to me? Who hit me? Are they coming back to finish the job? How did I get here?*

A nurse carrying a chart guided a blood pressure machine into the room. "Hello, I'm your nurse. How are you feeling? I need to take your vital signs and check your IV."

The nurse did not smile but proceeded to check his blood pressure, pulse, and monitors in the room.

"I am Betty, and I will take care of you this morning. Do you remember your name? Your date of birth? There are some items we need to record to register you."

"My name is Henry. Henry March. My date of birth is June 20, 1955. Now I have a question for you. How did I get here? What happened?"

Betty said, "Someone found you by the shore and brought you in. There was a nasty gash on your head. It looks like you got into a fight."

Henry tried to joke and say, "Yeah, you should see the other guy. Funny, but I don't remember a thing. Was I unconscious the whole time? Who found me?"

Betty did not answer any questions. Instead, she said, "The police want to question you on what happened. Are you up to talking to them?"

Henry pondered what to say. All he could feel was his pain and a bit of wooziness. "Can you give me something to help with the pain? I'm about to pass out!"

Nurse Betty said, "I can give you some ibuprofen. That should help."

"Sure. If you give me some aspirin, I'll tell the police what I know."

Nurse Betty said, "OK. I will bring them in. I will be right back."

The nurse left the room with the blood pressure machine. Henry remembered the lady in the water, and it all started returning to him. "I wonder what happened to the lady in the lake? Did they find out what happened to her? Who tried to kill her? Where's my dog? Somebody better have some answers!" he muttered, starting to panic again.

He thought back to when he saw the unfortunate lady. Henry was not a forensic doctor but could tell she must have taken some potent hallucinogens. The expression on her face seemed calm and drawn. Yet, her eyes appeared open. Her body was limp and lifeless. *Hmm, maybe I have missed my calling! I could be in one of those TV crime shows!* Henry thought.

Two police officers walked in. They stood on either side of Henry's bed. The taller of the two introduced them. "I'm Sergeant Jones, and this is detective Marshall. We are here to investigate a crime and need your help on this case," he said.

Detective Marshall looked at Henry. "What do you know about your attacker? Did you see him? Anything that might help us find them? Facial features? Walk? Language? What did they say?"

Henry said, "I don't remember anything. My dog started barking, and I woke up here. We had discovered something and called the police."

Detective Marshall said, "Why were you at the dockside at the lake this early morning? What were you doing? What did you see?"

Henry replied, "Well, my dog and I were just going for a walk when we found something strange in the water."

Sergeant Jones said, "Please tell us what you saw. We got a call from your phone number about a mysterious body that you found in the lake. Did you know the lady that you made the phone call about? What was your connection to her?"

Henry said, "I don't know her. I saw her in the water, and it looked like she was dead."

"She was in the water? We saw her on the beach."

Henry remembered his stupid thought of being heroic and remembered he had taken her out of the water. "Well, you see, I was being the good Samaritan and determining if she was dead. I immediately called the police. Ouch! My head! Where's my aspirin? Nurse!"

Nurse Betty brought Henry a paper pill cup with ibuprofen and a plastic cup filled with water. Henry swallowed the tablets and drank down the water.

He smiled at her gratefully. "Thanks!"

Nurse Betty smiled back and walked away.

"Her name was Martina Schwartz. From what I'm told, her friends called her Martie," said Detective Marshall.

Martina worked at the gallery on the East Side. She sold her sculptures for top dollars. Martina had been missing for a few days, and there was a missing person ad out for her."

Sergeant Jones took out a notebook. "There was a gala at the Madison Gallery, and celebrities were there. It started at seven. We were told there was someone that she was talking to that she was very fond of. He is one of our persons of interest."

Sergeant Jones pulled a photo from his pocket. "Have you seen this man?"

Henry looked at the photo of a handsome man with black hair, brown eyes, and a sturdy chin. He looked mean in the picture. Henry looked up at sergeant Jones. "I don't remember seeing anyone. I just thought someone needed to know that a woman's body was in the water. Didn't think I'd end up here!"

Henry shook his head as if to reinforce his words, "No, I can't say that I've ever seen him. Since I'm retired, I don't get out much. Wish I hadn't gone out today."

Then, Henry became curious. "I can't say that I've ever seen him. Thank God. He does not look like someone I would want to cross. Why do you think I would know him?"

Detective Marshall said, "No, you would have no reason to know him. He only associated with people on the upper east side, and his art was considered 'retro.' Not the kind of paintings that Martina would normally display."

Sergeant Jones scribbled something in the notebook. "She liked the classics, you know. Well, then again, I guess you wouldn't know. This was your first encounter with Martina Schwartz."

"Yeah, hopefully, my last!" said Henry.

"Maybe that was the one who hit you," said Detective Marshall, studying Henry surreptitiously.

Henry could feel the pain on the side of his head and called the nurse for some morphine. All he wanted was for the pain to go away and to try to sleep. Then, waking up and realizing that all this had been a nightmare.

Detective Marshall handed Henry a card. "If you remember anything else, let me know. And, let me give you a word of advice. Be careful who you play 'Good Samaritan' to. You were lucky this time."

Henry just grunted and looked at the detective. *Hindsight is easy, isn't it?* he thought. To the officer, he said, "I will."

The nurse walked in and added morphine to his IV. As the medication went through the veins in his arms, Henry drifted off to sleep.

***

Today, exactly one year ago, Martina fell in love with Felix Omar the minute she met him. His smile, defined chin, brown chestnut eyes, and Adonis physique intrigued and captivated her. His eyes were alluring and had a heavenly but naughty glow whenever Felix glanced at her. It was a lustful but tempting look that made Martina tingle.

Martina liked that he looked rugged, like Clint Eastwood or some Wild West cowboy. There was something about him that made her feel protected and sheltered. He looked like he had seen hard times, but they had not broken him. Then, there was his touch ....

The minute Felix touched her hand, she felt compelled to be close to him. He had this charisma, chemistry, and energy. Martina was drawn to him like a magnet.

Martina's fate crossed that of Felix Omar on the evening of the grand opening of her new showroom at Martina's Bella Donna Art Gallery.

She was busy talking to a prospective client when she noticed the man staring at her with a dark intensity. Martina was not very used to male attention – a previous love affair ended some years ago. Since then, she has immersed herself in her work.

Martina had worked hard to establish her Bella Donna Art Gallery as one of the best in the city. She was known for her exquisite taste and ability to find new and exciting artists.

The glamorous evening did justice to her and the gallery. It was a white tie and tails affair, with the who's who of the art scene and local celebrities attending. It kicked off with a Big Band to set the scene. As the evening progressed, a famous jazz musician was playing his tunes.

Martina was speaking to the owner of a large theatre downtown. The owner was considering adding murals to the walls encircling the amphitheater. Martina briefly looked at the strange man but then turned her attention back to the conversation. "So, there is a round stage in the amphitheater's center? This is really a unique opportunity," Martina said.

When she looked again, the man was gone. She briefly spoke to the mayor, who wanted to commission sculptures of historical figures for the State Capitol.

Martina was the perfect hostess, moving from guest to guest and chatting animatedly with everybody. She was taking a breather with a glass of water in hand when the strange man touched her arm.

"Excuse me, madam. Please allow me to introduce myself. I am Felix Omar," he said, his dark eyes framed with long lashes.

"Hello, Mr. Omar. I am Martina Schwartz," she said.

He took her outstretched hand and planted a light kiss on it. "Enchanté," he said.

"So, what do you do for a living, Mr. Omar?" Martina asked.

"I am an artist, and I think my work will be a perfect match for your gallery," he said.

Martina laughed, amused at his brazen confidence. He smiled, and his defined chin caught her attention. He held up a folder. "Here is my portfolio. I've done paintings, artwork, and advertising for some companies in the area. Any of these companies will give you a good reference regarding my work," he said confidently.

An old friend of hers interrupted their conversation. "Martie, you won't believe who also showed up tonight. Come with me ..."

"Mr. Omar, please excuse me. I have to go. Please phone me later," Martina said, turning around to follow her friend. She didn't see Felix Omar's eyes flash with anger, his friendly smile gone.

The rest of the evening went by in a whirl. Martina gave two television interviews, one for the news program on Channel 5 and the other for the Discovery Channel. Happy but exhausted, she waved goodbye to the last of her guests. Martina went back into the gallery, saying to herself, "For once, I can breathe and not worry about money."

She cleaned up the display area and put away the left-over bottles of wine. Her staff helped clean up the kitchen. Martina thanked them for their hard work and told everyone how pleased she was with how the night festivities went.

Just then, the phone rang. Martina sighed and answered, "This is Martina from Martina's Bella Donna Art Gallery. Can I help you?"

"This is Felix Omar. We met tonight at the gala?"

Martina had forgotten all about Felix and was ready to go to bed. However, he had not forgotten about her.

Martina took a deep breath. "Oh, yes. Hello, Mr. Omar. How can I help you?"

"Well, I was wondering when I could meet with you for our business meeting?"

Frowning, Martina said, "Ah, remind me what this is about?"

Felix was a little put off that she had forgotten. He attempted to maintain his composure. "We discussed what I could offer to your gallery."

Martina replied, "Well, I am very busy the next few weeks, but I might be able to fit you in at lunchtime next Tuesday afternoon. Shall we say 1 pm at the new French restaurant, Au Renoir Ma Belle?"

Felix said, "Isn't that where they serve snails?"

Martina rolled her eyes and said, "Yes, but it is called escargot. It is a delicacy. There is probably something you would find that you like."

"I was hoping we could go somewhere and get Philly sandwich on sourdough bread. However, French food it is," Felix said.

"I will pencil you in for next Tuesday afternoon. See you then."

"Until then, I will dream of a paradise with you."

"Excuse me? What did you just say, Mr. Omar?" Martina asked, irritation creeping into her voice.

"Nothing ... just a joke. I will meet you at the restaurant next Tuesday," Felix said.

Martina ended the conversation. "Dear Lord," she said to herself. "This guy is something else. Do I really want to meet with him?"

***

Forensic investigators were swarming all over Martina's home, checking for any clues on what had happened to Martina and how she ended up in the lake.

"Detective Marshall, I've found something," a police officer called, holding up a sheet of paper.

The detective walked to where the officer was looking through a stack of paperwork. He took the sheet and whistled softly when he started reading. "What do we have here? A lover's poem ..."

"When the time is right,
I will see you tonight
And pray that my dream will come true.
When I have to go away,
I will look for some way to meet somebody new.
I know that you're no good
But I keep wanting you.
I am not sure what I should do. I'm so afraid of you.
I know it's all wrong
But I know I belong.
Before my poor heart breaks in two.
I'm leaving you."

***

Felix arrived early at the Au Revoir Ma Belle and arranged for a corner table for two. He was armed with his portfolio, a huge bunch of red roses, and a box of chocolates.

Martina was a few minutes late and walked through the door. She was surprised when the head waiter showed her to a cozy table in the corner – the corner usually reserved for couples whispering sweet nothings to each other.

Felix jumped to his feet and pulled out her chair. "So good to see you again, Martina. I've taken the liberty of getting this table," he said.

Martina nodded. "Thank you. Did you bring your portfolio so I can see what you have to offer to my gallery?"

"Yes, I did," said Felix. I am sure you will be pleased with what I can offer."

Martina was not so sure ...

"I think my work could be displayed in the contemporary part of the gallery," he said, looking at her expectantly.

Martina studied the paintings and saw that they had some potential. She was taken by the contemporary abstract strokes in his work. "Mmm, I don't normally display this type of artwork, but I am open-minded and willing to see if there is a mutual profit for both of us," she said.

Felix smiled at her dazzlingly, and Martina felt butterflies flutter in her stomach. She berated herself silently when her cheeks warmed when he handed her the roses and chocolate with a gallant bow. *Martina, are you stupid?* she thought.

To her surprise, the meal was quite pleasant. She found herself laughing at his stories and anecdotes about prominent figures on the art scene.

Almost two hours later, she looked at her watch. "Well, Mr. Omar ... Felix, it was most enjoyable. However, I must get back to the gallery."

Felix replied, "How about I treat you to Starbucks and seal the deal?"

Martina smiled. "If you think that seals the deal you don't know much about business. I still have to discuss it with one or two investors. Let's meet again in a week."

Felix said, "That sounds fine."

He stood up, kissed Martina on the cheek, and left his portfolio on the table.

She watched him as he walked out of the restaurant. "There is something about him that does not seem right. I can't put my finger on it, but something is wrong here. I wonder if I am making the right decision to include him in my gallery," she muttered.

Another guest walked over to the table and introduced herself. "I am Sarah Roberts. I'm very pleased to finally meet you, Martina. I want to commission a portrait from you," she said.

Martina left the restaurant with Sarah, discussing the portrait. The going rate for her work was $1,000.00 a painting and Sarah was eager to pay the tab.

Well, if things with Felix didn't work out, there are always other possibilities, Martina thought.

***

Martina had a busy week at the gallery. The foreboding feeling about Felix left her mind. There were phone calls, an appointment at the mayor's home, a garden party, and a charity auction of one of her paintings.

Late on Monday afternoon, Martina enjoyed a cocktail with a visiting dignitary in town and talked about her views on politics. She was very knowledgeable when it came to current events.

When she returned to the gallery in the evening, Martina checked the gallery to make sure everything was immaculate. She was tired, but nothing a warm bubble bath couldn't fix.

It was 9:15 pm when she bolted the gallery doors behind her. Suddenly, a chill went up and down her back.

A figure rushed from the shadows, shouting angrily, "I thought that you would never come out! I've been waiting for you forever!"

It was Felix Omar. "You are mistaken, Mr. Omar. Our meeting is tomorrow afternoon. I do not recall making alternative arrangements," she said, anger taking the place of fear.

"But ... but ..." he started, still in a loud voice.

Martina interrupted him. "Really, Mr. Omar, I am having second thoughts. You are far too pushy and not showing any form of professionalism. I am not just someone you can pick up, and I don't appreciate you being so forward when I don't know you. I want to give you back your portfolio and forget the whole thing."

She opened the trunk of her car and handed back his portfolio. Her confidence returning, she continued in an icy tone. "If you want a business deal with me, that is not the way to greet me. So what were you doing hiding in the shadows? Were you trying to frighten me? Do I need to call the cops on you?"

Felix backed down and spread his hands in front of him. He smiled disarmingly. "I am sorry that you thought I was trying to frighten you. You are very thin-skinned. I will be more careful in the future. And I will double-check my diary. Am I forgiven?"

Martina nodded. "Yes, but don't ever do that again," she said, unlocking her car's door. "Now, if you will excuse me ..."

"Please, Martina, allow me to buy you dinner as an apology. I am really sorry," Felix pleaded. "I want to show you I'm not the abrasive man you think I am."

Martina shook her head. "Look, I'm tired. Let's reschedule tomorrow's meeting, and ..."

Felix said, "No, I'm starving. Tonight will work better for me."

Martina sighed. "OK, I will give you another chance, but you have made a terrible impression. I expect better treatment. I don't know you, and I would not even let my own family act like a jerk around me."

Felix backed off and said, "OK. Understood. Are we taking your car or mine?"

Martina was shocked by the question. *What nerve!* she thought. "I will drive myself and meet you there in five minutes. They should still be open. So I will see you there."

As Martina drove off, the artist, Felix Omar, watched her. He chuckled to himself.

"This one will be a challenge ... but so were the others. In the end, they had to submit. This one has grit, though. It will be fun taming her," he muttered.

***

Martina drove away, flushed with indignation. *He is arrogant and mean. Maybe I should go straight home and not meet with him at all?* she thought.

Then she gasped. "What if he follows me home and finds where I live? Time to set some ground rules quickly!" she muttered.

Martina drove into the parking lot of the French restaurant, Au Revoir Ma Belle. She got out of the car, surveyed the area around her, and locked the car doors. Felix was there already. He walked towards her car in a confident but thoughtful manner.

"Martina, or should I say, Ms. Schwartz, I realize that I behaved badly, and I apologize again for upsetting you," he said. "I am still new in business, and sometimes I forget my manners. I am used to working alone, so I don't have to answer to anyone."

Martina said cautiously, "OK, as I said, I will accept your apology. However, I cannot stay long. I am willing to listen to your business proposals."

Felix gave one of his dazzling smiles and took Martina's arm. "Let's start our relationship again," he said as they walked to the restaurant, holding the door for her.

He walked up to the hostess area and said, "I made reservations for 7:30 for two under the name Omar.

The waitress looked on the list and said, "Your reservations were for 7:30, sir. It's 9:25 pm!"

Felix looked very concerned and whispered to the hostess, "Here is something to keep our reservation open."

He handed the pretty young lady $40.00, looked into the girl's eyes, and smiled coyly.

The hostess smiled and said, "Right this way, Mr. Omar. Your table is ready."

Felix put out his hand to Martina and said, "Shall we?

Martina took his hand and followed him as if in a trance. Felix had charisma and appeared quite charming.

The hostess led them to the same corner table. This time, candles glowed in crystal globes. The band played smooth jazz while the clarinet player played familiar melodies. Martina couldn't remember the words of the songs and felt like she was dreaming.

The wonderful aromas from the kitchen reached their table. Martina eagerly glanced through the menu.

"What is your favorite wine, Martina? I will spare no expense to please you," Felix purred at her.

Martina's eyes widened. Why was he so persistent about a contract if he had so much money? she thought.

"I will take a Rose," she said, trying to suppress a feeling of unease.

Felix Omar got the waiter's attention and said, "A Rose for the lady and make mine a gin and tonic with a twist."

The waiter brought back the drinks and asked what Martina would like to order. Martina gazed again at the menu and said, "I would like the Coq Au Vin."

Felix said, "I will have the Boeuf Bourguignon."

"Excellent choices!" said the waiter.

"Excuse me for a moment," Felix said and rose from the table. He walked up to the band and spoke to the band leader. The band leader stopped the song they were playing and started playing a piece of music that was romantic, sensual, deliciously charming, and aesthetic to the ears.

Felix returned to the table, extended his hand, and said, "Martina Schwartz, shall we dance? My favorite song is playing."

Martina almost forgot where she was and why she had met Mr. Omar. She was just about to get up when a tiny little voice spoke in her mind. *Wasn't he going a little overboard with a business proposal? I mean, really?*

Martina snapped out of her dreamlike state. "No, I'm not here to dance, and I did not intend to stay long. Let me hear more about your business proposal."

Felix sighed and took his portfolio from his briefcase. Martina looked through his art again and read some of his reviews.

"Very impressive. But, our gallery does not have modern art. Impressionistic, maybe. But art decor, retro, no."

Felix persisted. "Just give me a small area, and I will work my magic around the room. I could use some publicity in this area."

Martina shrugged. "Well, what do we have to lose? I will let you display your art as long as you understand that it is temporary."

Felix grinned and said, "I think you will be surprised how many people like modern art."

The waiter came to the table and brought their food. "Bon Appétit."

The food was excellent, and Martina started to enjoy the evening. Suddenly, Felix raised his glass. "I propose a toast to a mutually successful partnership," he said.

Before Martina could raise her glass in response, Felix put his hand on hers and said, "I would like to see you again, Martina. If we work together, you will see a lot of me."

Martina cleared her throat. "You are getting forward again, Felix," she said.

Felix chuckled. "Guilty as charged. Forgive me, please, Martina," he said.

Martina changed the subject to Felix's magazine displays. "Where do you get your ideas, Felix? From old magazines from the 40s and 50s?" she asked.

"I get my ideas from many sources – all legitimate, of course," he replied, winking at her.

She laughed. "Well, I would hope so! Is there any copyright where these items cannot be used?"

Felix replied, "No, they're my own work."

Martina enjoyed the music and the conversation for the rest of the evening. "Well, Felix, I've stayed much longer than I anticipated. Time for me to leave," she said.

"That shows me you enjoyed the evening. I will walk you to your car," Felix said.

He followed Martina out to her car. Martina started feeling uneasy again.

"I wanted to make sure that you were safe. I hope I will see you soon," Felix said, looking at Martina expectantly.

Martina said, "Thank you for a lovely evening. I will call you soon about the contract. "

"I will look forward to your call. Until then, goodnight, Martina. You are as lovely as your name," Felix replied, looking at her with a strange, intense expression.

Martina felt embarrassed, and her cheeks were flushed. "Goodnight, Mr. Omar," she replied.

***

Felix drove home, humming the French song he requested from the band leader. He parked in the driveway and got out of the car. His footsteps and the turning of the key in the lock disrupted the silence.

Felix hung up his jacket and took off his shoes. In his bedroom, he changed into his comfortable pajama pants and tee-shirt. He walked into the kitchen to get a quick snack and something cold to drink.

As he opened the refrigerator door, he heard the voice again. It was a voice from the past, beckoning and taunting him, "Felix, where have you been? Felix, what have you done?"

He was frightened.

"It was just a business date. She means nothing to me. You know that I have only loved you," he said, pleading.

Felix covered his face with his hands, perplexed. *Why do I hear her voice in the kitchen? Does she have unfinished business that must be settled before her spirit can pass on? Why do I always hear my sweetheart calling me from this one spot on the kitchen floor?* he wondered, tears running down his face.

Then, he shouted angrily, "You're dead! Why do you haunt me?"

***

"Sergeant Jones, there is somebody here to see you about Martina Schwartz," a young officer announced.

Sergeant Jones looked up from his report. "Who is it?"

The officer replied, "It is a guy that works at the gallery. "

"Let him in," Sergeant Jones ordered.

A tall man, going prematurely grey, walked into the office. Sergeant Jones rose from his chair. "Good morning, sir. Christopher Jones. Pleased to meet you."

"My name is George Adamo. I worked with Martina Schwartz," he said. He sat down in response to Sergeant Jones' motioning to him.

"What can you tell me, George?" asked Sergeant Jones.

"I did not like Felix Omar from the moment I met him. I could tell he was up to no good," said George, looking angry.

"Who's Felix Omar?"

George scowled. "He was this prick pretending to be an artist. He got Martina to display his so-called art in the gallery."

Sergeant Jones motioned him to continue. "Felix flirted with the guests, and Martina would get very jealous. Girls would follow him around. Martina said they were just friends, but I could tell there was more going on. Every now and then, she would come to work crying but would not talk about it. Can I smoke?"

Sergeant Jones pushed an empty coffee mug towards George. "Go ahead," he says, making a mental note to wash the mug before the kitchen lady got hold of it.

"That night, Felix seemed out of sorts, and he started getting angry at her for her jealousy. He grabbed her by the arm and started talking to Martina in a bossy and dominating manner. He led her outside to talk. Martina tried to push Felix away. She told him that it was over. They started shouting and then went outside. They continued shouting, and then, after a while, Martina told me to close up shop. That was not like Martina. She was very OCD. She had to be the last person to lock up to ensure everything was in its place."

"How long have you known Martina Schwartz?" Sergeant Jones asked.

"For a few years – eight, nine? We were like brother and sister." His voice trembled, "I did not know that that night would be the last time I would see Martina."

"Did Martina tell you things about their relationship?" asked Sergeant Jones.

"Yeah. Felix Omar told her how he did not want her to date other guys. He was insanely jealous. "That night, Felix was very drunk and talking to her like she was a woman of the night. He called her all kinds of names. He was very mean and abusive. The bastard!" George growled.

He looked at Sergeant Jones. "Martina would tell me that Felix had a temper and to ignore him. But I knew better. He walked Martina out to her car, and that was the last I saw of her. I would say Felix is your prime suspect." "Where can we reach you, George?" Sergeant Jones asked.

George pulled out a card from his wallet. "Here's my card. Let me know how I can help. What a shame. The gallery was going so well."

Sergeant Jones walked him to the door. "I will pass the information to the lead investigator, Detective Marshall. Thanks for your help."

"Don't mention it," said George Adamo.

***

He started taking her on romantic outings and wanted Martina all to himself. No one could get close to her without Felix Omar snarling and making them go away. She was his.

When they danced, Felix held her so tightly that she couldn't breathe. She felt passion and desire but was afraid of her feelings for him. There was something about Felix that scared her.

Her intuition said, "Run away. You are going to get hurt." However, she was stuck like a fly in a spider's web.

On this particular evening, Martina sat across the table at a restaurant and listened to his words. She tried to concentrate on the conversation while wondering why she was there. How could such a man love her? Would things end up like they did in the past? A moment of fear overcame her.

Felix reached across the table and took her hand. "What is wrong, my beloved? You don't have to be frightened anymore. I will protect you," he said.

"I have a surprise for you, Martie," he said, beckoning to the waiter.

The waiter disappeared from view. After a minute, he came to their table, carrying a guitar.

Felix smiled. "Thank you, Emile. I've brought my guitar to serenade you."

He started strumming softly, and then started singing an old song called *Tu es la tentation* ('You are a temptation').

The melody was a song of his undying love with a fortissimo of melody, rhyme, and desire. Every note, chord, and variation to the melody was haunting and mesmerizing.

Martina closed her eyes and got lost in the music. After the last chord died away, she opened her eyes again. Felix put down the guitar and took her hand, looking at her with a slow fire in his eyes.

"Now the real song begins. Spend your life with me and make me the happiest man on earth. Marry me, my dearest Martie ..."

Martina's heart raced. Should she consider the proposal or run away? Her gut told her to run, but she firmly told the voice to be quiet.

***

George Adamo had not even left the building yet, when Sergeant Jones walked to Detective Marshall's office.

"I've just had a very interesting conversation with one George Adamo. He worked with Martina Schwartz. According to him, we should look no further than Felix Omar," Jones said.

Detective Marshall leaned back in his chair. "Now, isn't that interesting ... And who might this gentleman be?"

"An artist. He exhibited his work at Martina's gallery. But that's not all. Apparently, he and Martina were more than colleagues."

"Fantastic! Let's pay Eduardo and Josephine a visit. Maybe they can tell us more," said Detective Marshall.

They walked down the passage and entered the computer room. "Morning, you two. I need a favor, please. What can you tell us about Felix Omar?" asked Detective Marshall.

Josephine's fingers danced across her keyboard. "What do you know! Omar had a wife named Rachel," she exclaimed.

Eduardo looked up from his computer. "What happened to her?"

"She died five years ago of a brain hemorrhage. Trauma to her head. Mr. Omar said he came home and found her comatose. He called the police. When the police got there she had already passed on. Felix Omar was charged with her murder, but was eventually cleared. They never found the killer."

Detective Marshall and Sergeant Jones looked at each other. "Mmm ... can you find anything else about Rachel?" asked Sergeant Jones.

Eduardo looked up from his screen. "Her mother was very vocal about the court case at the time. It says here that she was convinced Omar did it. But there never was any proof," he said.

"I think we need to speak to her urgently," said Detective Marshall.

"How is the man who found Martina?" asked Josephine.

"He is getting better and ready to be discharged. His dog ran off, and no one has seen him. I wonder if the intruder got rid of the poor dog?" said Sergeant Jones. "But now, we must go."

Josephine was quiet. *How was this man with the head injury involved in all of this?* she wondered.

***

A soft rain was falling when Detective Marshall and Sergeant Jones knocked on the door of Rachel's mother. An elderly woman opened the door slightly. "Can I help you?"

"Good morning, madam," said Detective Marshall. "We are from the police department. We would like some information about your daughter and how she passed away."

The woman started shaking. "Come in. There is no one following you, is there?"

Sergeant Jones shook his head. "No, ma'am. No one followed us, but we need your help in a criminal investigation."

The elderly woman replied, "Come in but please close the door and lock it. You never know who might be listening. Are you sure you were not followed?"

"We weren't followed, but if it makes you feel better, you will get some police backup," replied Detective Marshall. Rachel's mother sighed. "After what I tell you, I might need it."

She started sobbing and grabbed her handkerchief. She led them into a tiny lounge, and they sat down. After a minute, the elderly woman regained her composure.

"Felix Omar said he came home from work at the usual time and found Rachel at the bottom of the stairs. She wasn't dead but was severely injured. She had bruises all over, and her head had several wounds. He said he called 911 and that she died before they arrived."

"So why did the police charge Omar with her murder?" asked Detective Marshall.

"Neighbors said they heard shouting earlier that day. They were convinced it was Omar and Rachel. They fought frequently. A man down the street said he saw Omar's car racing off. He even showed police his security camera footage. But the car's license plate wasn't clear, and he didn't take down the number. So we could never prove it. But he says it definitely was Omar."

Sergeant Jones was scribbling in his notebook. "Anything else, madam?" he asked.

"My husband never forgave Felix and vowed to make his life a living hell. Unfortunately, he fell ill shortly after Rachel's death. He couldn't get over her passing. I think he died of a broken heart," she said, tears running down her cheeks again.

Detective Marshall frowned. "We are very sorry for your loss, madam."

Rachel's mother looked at him. "But why are you asking me these questions? Did another woman get killed?"

Sergeant Jones replied, "A woman named Martina Schwartz was found in the lake at a nearby park. Ms. Schwartz was Felix Omar's love interest. A retired gentleman was walking his dog and found her. Got knocked on the head for doing a good deed. No good deed goes unpunished!"

Rachel's mom sat down and held her stomach. She started talking in an unintelligible manner. Then she said, "He ran, didn't he?"

Detective Marshall sighed, "Yeah, he ran. But we are looking for him."

Rachel's mother said, "You will find clues in his paintings. He leaves messages somewhere in his artwork. I found that out after Rachel's funeral. He is a dangerous man!"

Detective Marshall and Sergeant Jones got up to leave. Sergeant Jones looked at the elderly woman with sympathy. "The case is under investigation, madam. We will do our best."

Just before she closed the door, she said, "Please catch him. Please make him pay for my daughter's death and this poor girl in the lake."

***

Felix Omar sat on the couch in front of his TV, eating dinner and watching a music program. Suddenly, a 'Breaking News' bulletin interrupted the program.

"A suspect was identified in the attack on Martina Schwartz, the owner of a well-known art gallery in the city. Ms. Schwartz sustained severe injuries and is still in a coma," the announcer said.

Next, Felix Omar saw his face on the screen. "This man is Felix Omar. If you see him, call the Crime Stoppers number at 888-777-3033. He is considered very dangerous. Do not try to apprehend him."

Felix jumped to his feet. He rushed to the kitchen and vomited into the kitchen sink. Then, he started pacing the kitchen floor and muttering, "Rachel, they think I tried to kill her! I am a suspect in Martina's case! The police are looking for me!"

A ghostly image appeared and said, "Why are you running? You are guilty, aren't you?"

Felix said, "You know it was an accident that happened to you, don't you? I really did not kill you!"

"I know you tried to save me," Rachel said softly.

Felix's voice became more urgent, "Yes, I did! You slipped. Well, you remember what happened. But I didn't try to kill Martina Schwartz!"

Rachel asked quizzically, "Then who did, Felix? Maybe you need to backtrack your steps and figure out who might have wanted Martina killed."

"Rachel, it wasn't me!" Felix looked at Rachel accusingly and said, "Maybe it was you!"

Rachel scoffed. "Brilliant, Felix! As if I could drug her and put her in the water. You know better than that!"

Felix looked like a petulant child. "Well, she isn't dead!"

Rachel laughed. "At least you're not guilty of murder!"

Felix felt a chill go up and down his back.

"But they are still looking for me. There is a manhunt out for me. Rachel, what should I do?" he cried.

Rachel faded away, and Felix hung his head in despair. "I'm alone in this. Trapped like a rat! I've got to get out of here!" he shouted.

He rushed to his bedroom and started piling clothes into a suitcase. Suddenly, he saw bright lights. Police cars were starting to pull into his driveway. One of the cops got out a loudspeaker. "Come out with your hands in the air! We know you're in there!" he shouted.

Felix didn't know whether to shoot or to run. He rushed back to the kitchen and opened the back door. Too late, the house was surrounded.

Felix walked out with his hands in the air. "I didn't do it! I am innocent," he cried.

Detective Marshall walked up to him. "Felix Omar, you are being arrested for the attempted murder of Martina Schwartz. Everything you say will be held against you. You have a right to an attorney," he said.

Felix felt as if he was dreaming. The cop's words just melted into the air. They took him by the arm and walked down the driveway. Next, he felt someone shoving him into the backseat of the squad car.

He looked out the window and saw Rachel. "It's your turn to pay, Felix!" she said. Then, her image disappeared into the night.

Felix's eyes widened. *Who has it out for me? Was it me? I don't remember anything anymore*, he thought as the police car drove off.

***

Felix Omar was found guilty on all counts. He pleaded insanity and was diagnosed with severe schizophrenia. He did not remember what he did when his other personalities took over. He was sentenced to a lengthy prison term on the island of Desprey, in an old prison built in 1851.

When he was thrown into his cell, he heard the voices of all the women that he had killed. He screamed, but no one came to his rescue.

***

Martina eventually woke up from her coma and told the police about the erratic and frightening things Felix would do. She was assured that he would never be free again.

Henry March was reunited with his dog. He had run home, and a neighbor was taking care of Marco. Henry received good medical treatment and was one of the key witnesses to Felix's sentence. It had been Felix Omar, or one of his personalities, that had knocked him out.

***

Martina decided to work hard to restore her business. She appointed security guards to check visitors who came into the gallery. She completed the commissions that she had agreed to do. Keeping busy took her mind off her problems, at least temporarily.

Her friend, George Adamo, sat with her in court when the verdict was delivered. They decided to close up shop for two weeks. They went to Paris for a romantic rendezvous, putting the past behind them.

***

Felix Omar can appeal his sentence in 50 years....

Table of Contents

The Winter Winds Prevail

She dances in a circle to a tune that's in her head. She goes back to her memories of a book that she once read.

No one really knows her
or what is on her mind.
She is looking for answers.
She is looking for a sign.

She walks with broken pieces.
Yet she starts to blaze a trail
for those who try to be with her.
The winter winds prevail.
No one really knows her
or what she has in mind.
She is looking for answers.
She is looking for a sign.
(Repeat last verse)
For a sign
For a sign
For a sign.

The Locked Box
Series

The Locked Box

Norma's Story

Norma was in 4th grade in her homeschool studies. She lived in Granite City with her mom and dad and was an only child. Norma felt special being the only child. Her mom spent time with her when her dad would go to work. They drew pictures together in sketchbooks and would laugh at the funny characters they could draw. Lisa and Norma would swing on the swings, go to the park, go bowling, skate, and go to plays.

One night, Tony, her dad, entered the front door and started talking to Lisa. Tony asked Norma to come into the living room. Norma sat down.

Dad said, "We are separating. You will live with your mom, but I won't be here."

Her mom and dad separated, and Norma and her mom needed to move to an area where her mom, Lisa, could find employment. They lived in a small farming community, and there were few jobs.

Lisa did not have much education but she did the best she could to provide for Norma. Lisa found employment working at a hotel, cleaning rooms, and doing laundry.

They found an apartment and settled in. The hardest part was finding a new school. Norma had been homeschooled, so she did not know how to relate to kids' behavior in the public school environment.

Norma liked learning, and her mother explained the lessons in ways she could understand. Norma was above her current grade level in her studies.

Norma did not take the separation and divorce well. She ended up staying with babysitters while her mom worked.

Norma started retreating into a very comfortable and safe place in her mind. A place where people got along and life was happy. The place where she went when she drew pictures with her mom. Norma created characters to live in that world. When her mom was gone they would talk to her and play games. Mom was always tired, but Norma entertained herself with sketching.

The first day at the new school was strange. Her mom prepared her lunchbox and gave her some money for milk and cookies. Norma walked around for quite some time before finding her classroom. She was a country girl and did not wear the kind of clothes the other kids wore. Hair in braids, freckles on her face, and a simple dress with socks and tennis shoes.

The girls in the class started whispering about her, and Norma felt shy. She had never been in this situation before. Mom had always been there. Now there was no one to protect her. Norma opened up her sketchpad and started drawing.

One of the girls, Cherry, started making fun of Norma. "Look at those stupid drawings! I bet she thinks she can draw!" she said.

One of Cherry's crowd just watched and looked concerned. Her name was Debbie. The bell rang, and Norma tried to concentrate on the teacher's words.

Norma liked her teachers but was not sure about the kids she was in class with. Paranoia and worry set over her, and Norma hoped it was not obvious how her classmates were affecting her. Running away was not an option. Norma tried to ignore the other children and sat quietly during class.

During lunchtime, she sat on a bench and she got out her lunchbox and sketchpad. She drew pictures of the characters that were having a conversation in her head. Cherry and her friends started whispering about Norma. Then they started making fun of her.

Debbie, said sternly, "She's just drawing. Leave her alone!"

The girls started snickering and walked away. "Debbie, are you coming?" asked Cherry.

Debbie said, "In a minute. You can go on without me."

Debbie walked over to the bench where Norma was sitting and sat down. Norma had been listening to what Cherry and her friends were saying. She curled up into a shell. She closed her sketchpad and started holding her knees and rocking back and forth.

Debbie tried to talk to her, but Norma had already retreated into a different world, a different dimension in her head, so she could not be reached. In that world, no one had to explain why you were different. No one had to look the same or be accepted to survive. Norma started talking to her invisible friends and started eating her lunch. Debbie realized that once more, Norma had gone into her own 'locked box' and thrown away the key.

"What are you drawing? Can I see?"

Norma asked Debbie, "Why do you want to see it?"

Debbie said, "I wanted to say I'm sorry how Cherry and the gang treated you. That was not right. I want you to know that I don't like how you were treated and would like to be your friend. You can trust me. I will never hurt you.

Norma timidly opened her sketchbook and showed Debbie her vibrant and colorful characters.

"How do you do that? The characters are dancing! Do you have a computer program or app that helps you to draw so well?"

"No, this is a secret I learned from my mother. She is an artist."

"Does she sell art in town?"

"No, she doesn't." Norma started feeling insecure again and said, "I need to go. I've got to get to class."

Norma got her sketchpad, lunchbox, and books. She said a quick "bye" to Debbie and walked away.

Around the corner, Cherry and her friends were standing by and talking.

"So, Debbie, what did you learn about Norma? What's wrong with her?" asked Cherry.

Debbie shook her head and said, "I'm puzzled. She can make her drawings dance! She draws them, and then they dance! It is like they come alive for her!"

"They don't really dance, Debbie! Don't let Norma rub off on you. I knew there was something strange about that one!"

Debbie said, "Why do you have to be so mean to Norma? Leave her alone. She's done nothing to you."

"What's wrong? You suddenly sympathizing with that weirdo?"

"She's not weird. She's smart and artistic. To tell you the truth, I would rather be friends with her than you losers!"

"You're gonna regret that, Debbie, when it comes to cheerleading tryouts!"

"I'll take my chances," said Debbie, and she walked towards the classroom.

Debbie noticed Norma was talking to her imaginary friends. She had gone back into her locked box and was oblivious to what was happening around her. She was happy and accepted in her locked box, and did not have to worry about abuse or what others said.

Norma walked into the classroom, sat in her seat, and thought about her characters. Nothing could hurt her in her box. No person or thing was allowed to get in. It was a strange kind of safe but it was a world to herself. Her own locked box.

Debbie became a friend to Norma and formed their own group. Norma taught Debbie to discover and explore art and mathematical patterns with symmetry and balance. The basics of learning, the rhythm and rhyme of music, and the mathematics behind it.

The new group included those that were considered misfits to everyone else. Everyone had their own locked box. The only way the box could be opened was with a special key of communication.

Debbie and Norma's friendship lasted for years.

Lisa started selling her artwork and was hired on at a gallery. She did not have to work as many hours and enjoyed having Norma's friends over.

Norma had not realized mom had her own locked box. Lisa did not want Norma to think anything was wrong. She was hurting and not used to working outside the home. She kept her pain locked up. However, Lisa was inspired watching Norma and realized it was time for her to get back into her art. Norma's courage was just what she needed to make her dreams come true.

The Locked Box

Joe Barone's Story

Joe Barone was well-known for his musical style and skills. He was brought up in Chicago, Illinois, and worked his way up into 'fortune and fame.' All a person had to do was say his first name, and the image behind the name appeared. He could play the piano with the sweetest jazz you ever heard. Joe Barone was one of those musicians that you had to see to believe anyone could play with such style and majesty of the keyboard. Joe was known internationally as the jazz maestro.

Years of playing music, women, wine, and song were starting to wear on him, and Joe wondered where he went wrong.

True friends were hard to come by. However, they came around when there were money, parties, or photo shoots. Joe decided to go for a walk and found an old church with stained glass windows. Out of curiosity, Joe decided to walk in. The church reminded him of his childhood.

The virtuoso of song sat in the pew, bowed his head, and said prayers to the God that had seemed distant in his life. He thought of his 'rise to the top,' and realized that life was not as glamorous as he was told. No longer were you just a man. You were just an image, almost an illusion.

Therefore, the public could decide whether they like you or not based on the latest reviews.

A little boy walked into the hallowed church and noticed the famous singer. The child appeared to be an admirer of Joe. The kid was dressed in clothes from the 70s and looked out of place.

Joe noticed the child, nodded his head, and walked towards the windows in the church. The two met as they gazed upon the stained glass holy figures in the church windows.

Joe was curious but irritated that this child kept staring at him. Joe said, "Can I help you?"

The boy smiled, looked up at Joe's face, and said, "I want to be just like you!"

The singer smiled and saw on the child's face the dream of becoming something more than could be imagined.

No one was in the front part of the church. Joe walked past the pews and noticed a grand piano. In reverence, he sat down and played a jazz rendition of Just a closer walk with thee on the piano keys. Joe expected the child to clap or give some sort of praise.

The child looked up at Joe and said, "I bet I know why you are here. You seek peace away from the noise, drama, and confusion. I bet these feelings surround your life."

Joe was curious but perturbed that this child would try to get into his head. Joe said, "Just because I am playing in a church, you think you can psychoanalyze me?"

The singer bent down to the child's level and said, "You look familiar. Do I know your parents?"

The little child said, "Yes, you do. You know all of my histories, for this is where we cross paths. I am your dreams, hopes, and desires. In other words, I am you before you became famous."

Joe looked at the little boy and got a feeling of déjá vu. Joe put his hand on his face and shook his head.

Who the heck is this kid anyway? he thought.

Joe got up, turned away from the child, and faced the stained glass windows. Then he looked directly into the eyes of the little boy.

"There was a time I did not worry about anything. I played music, hoped for my songs to get out there, and lived the dream. I did not realize that I was living the dream when I was with the people who really loved me.

"It was fun at first with the lights, the fame, and the adoring fans. Then came the paparazzi. The calls, fake news, and the phobia every time the doorbell rang."

Joe tried to change the subject and asked, "So kid, what's your story?"

The little boy smiled and said, "I have been hiding; I have been kept away and put in this dark place, like a box. A secluded place where there was no light. I could not break free until now."

The singer said with curiosity and wonder, "How did you escape?"

The little boy said, "It was when you remembered me and let me out."

Joe said, "I let you out? What are you talking about?"

The child said, "Yeah, you finally let me out! I am the one that you have kept in the Locked Box."

Joe looked at the little boy and asked quizzically, "So, what do I call you – little Joe?"

The boy showed quick wit and said, "Do I look like I am Joe Cartwright in *Bonanza*? No, I am who you were when you dreamed about becoming the musician you are now."

Joe said, "OK, what happened? When did I become part of the corporate world and stop being the dreamer and the free thinker?"

The little boy said, "It was when you first signed your name on the contract with the record company and forgot to read the fine print."

Joe said, "Why do I need to read the fine print? That is what attorneys are for!"

The little boy said, "You forgot to read the part that says they own you. Your music, your words, your time, talent, and eventually your soul."

Joe said, "That is rather dramatic, don't you think?"

The little boy pulled a document out of his pocket signed by Joe.

"Here's the contract that you signed, Joe. This is where it all began."

Joe said sarcastically, "OK, little Joe. Give me the rundown! I'm dying to know what you can tell me that would change anything."

Joe's younger self said, "Let's simplify things. Call me Joseph, and I'll call you Joe. Deal?"

"Deal."

"OK. This is where it started ..."

***

Joe practiced with his piano teacher, Mrs. Humphrey. She was very strict and made sure Joe did not hit a wrong note. If he did, Joe had to practice the same lesson over and over again.

Joe almost gave up on learning. He would rather be playing softball or hockey.

During one of his lessons, a mother knocked on the door and asked to speak to Mrs. Humphrey.

"Joe, keep practicing," Mrs. Humphrey said.

She walked towards the door and opened it. "Hello, can I help you?" she asked.

"I heard that you give piano lessons to children. My daughter is six years old and I want her to learn how to play the piano."

Mrs. Humphrey replied, "Well, we have an opening for a new student. This is Joe Martuzi. He is one of my students. Let me show you some of the curriculum."

Mrs. Humphrey turned toward the little girl. "Have you played any piano before, dear?"

"No, madam, I haven't, but I'm willing to try," the girl said.

"What is your name?" Mrs. Humphrey asked with a friendly smile.

"Marjorie Watkins, madam," the girl said.

"Joe, would you like to play something for our new student, Marjorie?" Mrs. Humphrey asked.

Joe couldn't take his eyes off the pretty girl. He said, "Ah, I can play this tune."

He proceeded to play Twilight Time by The Platters. This was one of his favorite tunes and was easy to play. Joe played it so melodically that even Mrs. Humphrey clapped.

"Well, I must say, that song is not in our curriculum, but if you practice, maybe Joe can teach it to you," she told Marjorie.

"In the meantime, you will be practicing scales, doing drills, and working on the beginning piano book. I will expect you to practice two hours every day."

Marjorie's mom asked her daughter, "Are you willing to commit the time to practice and come for piano lessons?" Marjorie replied, "Yes, I can do this."

Joe was very impressed with Marjorie's level of confidence, considering she had never played. He decided there and then to continue with his music and get better.

Through the years, Marjorie and Joe became great friends. It looked like it was going to lead to something. She became a virtuoso on the piano and played classical music. Joe started listening to Duke Ellington, Louie Armstrong, and Fats Waller. He wanted to imitate their sound and style. He stopped taking lessons but continued in the band, concert orchestra, and playing for social events.

One day, Joe sat in the audience when Marjorie played Romeo and Juliet. His heart started racing, and his eyes lit up when Marjorie gazed at him during the song. Suddenly, he knew he had a chance.

Joe started playing with jazz bands all the time. His high school teachers had to wake him up during classes because the bands played so late.

Marjorie loved Joe and thought of the future that they had had together. She made money playing at the roller skating rink and at garden clubs.

Joe played wherever there was an opportunity. Somehow, he passed high school.

Marjorie was a year behind Joe in school and attended his graduation. She sat with Joe's mama and her mama.

After graduation, Joe took Marjorie for a drive to Lover's Point.

"Marjorie, you know I love you, but I've got a gig that will take me away for a few weeks. This man at the club came up to me and said he worked for a record company. If I signed a contract, I could start performing and getting the big bucks," Joe said.

Marjorie was heartbroken. "What about us? What am I supposed to do while you are off at your gig?" she asked, close to tears.

"Just wait for me. When I get enough money, I will send for you and, who knows? Maybe get married?"

Marjorie had dreamed of a proposal, but she hoped that he would follow through when he was done with his gig.

"I will wait for you, Joe," she said sadly.

Joe did not realize that the contract's small print demanded that he does much more concerts at parks, county fairs, and events around the country. His producer said, "Joe! You are going to be a big name."

Unfortunately, nothing much happened till Joe changed his name from Joe Martuzi to Joe Barone. He saw that name on an Italian restaurant somewhere.

As it turned out, Marjorie got the hint that Joe wasn't coming back soon. So, she met someone else that was playing in the symphony. He was a classical guitar player, James Hawkins. When Joe got the wedding invitation, he was sad but too busy to do anything about it.

Marjorie got married, and Joe played with the band.

***

Joe Barone contemplated all Joseph had said. "Now, here I am. I have gone through several bands, and we are still playing. This has become all I know. Is it too late to teach an old dog new tricks?"

Joseph smiled. "Well, you're not under contract. You have gold and platinum albums because of all the record albums you have sold. Plus, you played at Carnegie Hall and in Hyde Park. You are a star! What else do you want, Joe?"

"I want my life back. A quiet life. No paparazzi. Walks on the beach. Settling down with one woman and having a good life," replied Joe.

"So, you are willing to leave it all behind?" asked Joseph.

"No, I just want to play only when I want to. Sing when I want to and retire."

Joseph smiled. "In case you're interested, one of your other fans is here to see you."

Joe looked towards the door and saw a glimpse from the past, Marjorie.

Marjorie was older but still as beautiful as he had remembered.

"Hello, Joe. Do you remember me? I am here to lead you to the other side," she said. "You have smoked your last cigarette, drank your last beer, and played your last show. The curtain is coming down, and if you keep on the way you've been, it will be time to meet your maker. I am here with encouragement from your family to intervene for you."

Joe looked shocked. "I can't change, Marjorie. I am very set in my ways. Are you still with that guy you married?"

"No, Joe. I had cancer and died two years ago. I have come back to help you. Your mother has been praying for you to live a good life and to be happy. Your mom is getting old and wants to see you before she dies," said Marjorie.

"Marjorie, I want to see you on the other side where heaven is," Joe said, reaching toward Marjorie.

"I missed you, but life goes on. You need to go on too, Joe. People remember your name when you make laugh or join in a song. They forget you just as easily, Joe, because fame is fickle. It lasts for a moment and ends with flickering candlelight. Make peace with yourself, Joe. Do that for me."

Joe had tears in his eyes as she vanished.

He turned toward Joseph. "I will take her advice. Joseph, what do I do now?"

"Come back home. Start again. Find yourself and rise like a phoenix," Joseph said.

"I don't know," Joe said, shaking his head.

"But you have got to try!" Joseph exclaimed.

Joe decided to come out of the locked box and go home. To live a simpler life and meet someone who was like Marjorie. He was finally free of the locked box!

Janie's Story

When Janie was a little girl, food was part of a celebration. It was used in happy times. It was used to make up for sad times. It made her feel better when the neighborhood children made fun of her. It was something Janie could share when she learned to cook with her mom. Food was a comfort. A reward for getting through your week.

Food was more than survival – it was a lifestyle. Every day began and ended with food. However, it was a catch-22. When Janie looked in the mirror, she saw the results of her quest for food. The scale did not lie. She was over 200lbs and saw the reality of the illusion. Inside, Janie was a girl with talents, abilities, and gifts. No one could see what she had to offer. All that could be seen was a fat girl in the 'locked box' she had created.

Well-meaning people make it sound so easy. Just exercise and lose weight. Don't eat so much! If only it was that easy. Any addiction is hiding an underground purpose. To resolve any issue, you have to know the cause. Learn where the real hurt is. Find out what that addiction is doing for you. Then, learn how to find something that can take its place. Unless you find something to replace the need, you will return to it. Food an addiction? Yes! When it is used as a coping mechanism, it becomes an addiction.

Janie felt rejection and loneliness. She did not like herself, and her self-esteem was low. Janie did not have the energy or vitality and was tired all the time. She did not have many friends. Janie did not want to be seen in a bathing suit or anything revealing her weight. She stayed at home and watched the world from her bedroom window. Depression hit her, and she sank into her box away from the world. In that world, no one could hurt her. She closed the door and threw away the key.

After anti-depressants, anxiety medication, and off-the-counter weight control pills, she ended up in the hospital with a sudden heart attack.

Her only recourse was to lose weight or be on medication with several side effects. Janie decided that enough was enough. It was time to open the locked box for good.

She made some life changes. It was not easy. She had to come to terms with what she had done to her body. No one had to tell her, even though several that did. She started tracking what she ate. Then, she circled what she ate that was causing her to gain. Writing down what she ate made Janie think about what was being put into her mouth.

She got an exercise tape and practiced the steps with the teacher. She decided to keep track of her exercise activities as well. Janie did not write a weight down that she wanted to be. Janie's goal was that she wanted to be 5 lbs less. When she lost 5 lbs, she wanted to be 10 lbs less. This was her personal victory. No one noticed until she lost 50 lbs – quite discouraging, but to be expected. Janie found a way to deal with the hurt. She wrote in a journal and 'punched out her hurt feelings of rejection' with her exercise routines. As a result, the box was no longer closed. She felt more confident and sure of herself. Janie started joining clubs that matched her interest.

Janie did not know it, but many students at the school had their own locked boxes for coping. Janie decided her life goal was to help others like her. Help others see more than what was on the surface and beyond the locked boxes.

Janie had been there. Until you have been there, the enclosure is hard to understand. Understanding what could drive a person to stay inside the 'locked box.'

The Strange Customs of Wayward Ville

Lucy lived in a town where people had a strange way of dealing with people's problems. The place was called Wayward Ville. When someone had a problem, or if someone was having a bad day, they would follow an old custom. They would throw toilet paper or lemons at the person or persons.

When this happened, a person had a few choices. You could stock up (you never know when you might run out). You could make lemonade (try to make the best out of the situation). You could throw the toilet paper and lemons back (which could be a big mess), or just don't tell others your problems (keep them to yourself).

Lucy had the worst week of her life. She noticed nothing turned out right. She was late for work for two days because traffic was at a standstill. She had trouble completing her projects, burnt her dinner, and never had enough money to pay her bills. Things never worked out the way it was supposed to.

Unfortunately, the townspeople threw things at her (even though she didn't mention the kind of problems she was having).

Lucy started thinking about this custom. She asked a townsperson that had been there for years and years to explain the custom to her.

He said, "The toilet paper was for when things happen you did not plan for – when life is hard. The lemons are when you feel the situation really feels like lemons and life is sour to you."

She said, "Why is it people don't have sympathy anymore? Where did the caring go?

The man said, "We care about ourselves. We don't have time to care about other people. We use the toilet paper and lemons to tell people it's their problem, not ours."

Lucy understood now why this custom had been invented. She decided to start a petition to see if this custom could stop. She wanted to see if anyone else wanted to stop this silly custom.

She went door to door in her neighborhood. Lucy asked, "How do you feel when people throw these things at you?"

The neighbors said, "It makes us more self-centered. We don't care about other people. It keeps us from talking with others."

Lucy asked, "Do you believe in this custom?"

"No," said her neighbors.

They signed the petition. Lucy brought the petition before the city council.

"Most of the town's people don't believe in this custom. It should be stopped," she announced.

The councilman said, "But we have always done things this way. That way, no one bothers anybody."

Lucy said, "There is a better use for these things than using them to get your point across. Why not use them for good? When life hits the fan, you need someone to care. Not just think of themselves. You want to know you are heard. When you have a bad day, you need more than lemons. You might need a helping hand. You might need someone to listen or encourage you. When people don't listen and only want to talk about themselves, no one wins in the conversation. Even the one that is thinking just of themselves doesn't win. No one wants to talk to them. No one wants to hear them bragging on themselves."

The City Council put it to a vote. It was unanimous that the custom needed to be changed. It was agreed that people would not throw things when others were having a bad day. They would either give them space, or take time to listen.

Some townspeople did not agree with this ruling. They liked putting others down to build themselves up. However, they were overruled.

Lucy began to like this town again. She was able to talk to the townspeople. Even if she had a bad day, she was treated respectfully. When life hit the fan or gave lemons, there were better ways to deal with the stress and problems. People started showing more compassion and concern.

At the next Council meeting, they decided they were no longer wayward. They decided they needed to change their name. That was a front-page story. However, that story I will save for another day.

Mysteries of the Mind and the Shadows

Behind the Door Danger Waits

My name is Victoria. I am facing my greatest fear. Why tonight of all nights? I hear a noise. A large crash in the middle of the night. I am waking from a dream. I am trying to process that there is a sound, and I need to do something about it.

My imagination starts playing tricks on me. Is there someone in the house? What will I do if there is? How do I protect myself? How did he, she, or … it … get in? I locked all the doors myself! Is there someone behind the door waiting for me? I start to get afraid. Maybe I might not like the answer.

I try to reason with myself. *It was just a dream. Calm down*, I think. Maybe I ate something I shouldn't have. No one is in the house – I just imagine things. I try to go back to sleep. Another crash and the sound of a loud voice in the den. The voice sounds upset and unfamiliar. I sit up in my bed, and my heart is frozen with fear.

I am awake enough to realize that I am not dressed for meeting a stranger. Sparky, my dachshund, starts barking. Immediately, my puppy jumps into action to find the intruder.

I look for something to protect myself. Where is the baseball bat? But why would I keep sports equipment in my bedroom? I put on some sweat pants and a sweater. There is arguing and footsteps in the kitchen. Then, I hear a door opening.

Sparky runs to the front room barking, and then it turns quiet. No more scuffing paws on the living room floor. It is suddenly too quiet. My stomach starts to feel sick. What happened to my dog? Who is in the kitchen?

I must confront my intruder! He, she, or … it … is not welcome here! At last, I find my flashlight and a baseball bat. I take a deep breath and call 911 with shaking hands. "Dispatch, there is a prowler in my house!" I whisper urgently.

I give them my address. They would be here in 15 minutes. More voices. I can hear a dog barking outside. My upright piano is being played in harsh sharps and flat notes. What is going on? I am just starting my day, but I am ready for it to end!

More barking outside. Sparky is out and running after something! I am still sitting on my bed, wondering what to do and trying to devise a plan of action. Somehow, my fear is slowly turning into anger. How dare this person wake me up and stress me out? I need to find a means of escape! Then I need to make sure this person never messes with me again!

At this point, I start panicking again. I wish this were just a dream!

Please! Let me wake up from my frightening reality! I hear footsteps and they are getting louder!

The doorbell rings, and my dog runs out of the fence to greet whoever is at the door. The phone rings. It is a telemarketer who wants me to buy some timeshares. "I can't talk now," I say and hang up the phone abruptly.

My mind imagines the worst possible scenarios. Could the telemarketer really have been the person or persons that broke into my house? Could he or she have called to see if I was at home? Should I go out to the front room to see if I imaged things?

I open a bottle of water and try to drink it. My hands are shaking so much that I spill water on myself. *Oh now, I need the bathroom*, I think. The doorbell is still ringing.

I creep out of the room and walk slowly towards the front room – scared yet determined that I will not be afraid. Then I discover to my shock and dismay …

The TV is on, and an old cops and robbers story is playing! Did the TV turn itself on? My cat is playing on the piano keys and making a terrible sound! I walk towards the piano and trip over a suitcase. I fall to the floor. A book falls from a shelf above my head and hits me. I look around. Who left a suitcase here?

The side door is slightly open. I look around the house, and I don't see anyone. I carefully look behind doors and into the closets. My heart trembles with fear and confusion. The curtain rustles. Is that the form and reflection of a man?

The doorbell is still ringing and Sparky is still barking …. I cautiously open the door. It is a police officer.

"I am Captain Juniper. You made a call about an intruder. Are you Victoria Sights?" he says.

"Yes, officer. I called," I say in a croaking voice.

The officer takes out his notebook and pen. "What happened?"

My heart is thumping. Then I say, "Someone was talking loudly and turned on the television. I was asleep, but then I heard the door open. I saw the form of someone behind the curtain. Whoever is in the house left their suitcase!"

I open the door and let Captain Juniper in.

"Apparently, they were preparing to stay!" says Captain Juniper. "Let me check out who is behind the curtain! Before I do this, I will check out the suitcase."

The captain opens the suitcase and then looks at me.

"Do any of these items look familiar? Who might have access to your property?"

I gasp and shudder. "My old boyfriend! But I was told he destroyed the key! He was very angry when he left!"

I am trembling with fright. Why would Gerald, my old boyfriend, return? I know it is not for a good reason.

Captain Juniper says, "It looks like he planned to make a surprise visit. Calm down, Ms. Sights. I will check behind the curtain."

He gets to his feet. "By the way," Captain Juniper continued, "Is this your dog? She seemed eager to meet me. We became friends while waiting for you to open the door!"

I smile apologetically. "This is Sparky! She is my protector. My best friend."

Captain Juniper walks into the spare room. There is something behind the curtain. Slowly, he pulls it back –a broom, nothing else. Captain Juniper is perplexed and looks around the room, checking under the bed, in the closets, and corners.

"No sign of an intruder! There is no one in here. I am going to check around the house," he says.

The captain checks the kitchen, living room, bathroom and dining area. Finally, he goes to my room. "Ms. Sights, I found something!" he shouts.

I tremble, gulp, and hold my breath. Cautiously, I walk toward my room.

"There are pink and red hearts on your bed and a trail of red roses. Whoever was here must have left when I came in," he says.

I sit on my bed with my hand to my mouth. Who was here? Who would wake me in the middle of the night? Why were they trying to frighten me?

Suddenly, the captain points to the door of my closet. There was a large, red heart taped to it. I read the note in fear and terror.

"Until next time, Cherie. Remember, I am only a step away from your greatest fear."

The Justification for a Murder Mystery

The fog was intense and mystifying as Gerald Ratifier walked down the cobblestone streets towards his next appointment. The intruder's black trench coat had small drops of blood on the lapel that were hard to conceal. Gerald, the former lover of Ophelia, had convinced himself that he had cleaned up the evidence and that no one would know. It was a perfect crime because if anyone would be suspected it would be the housekeeper. She had just been in the guest room before the murder. No one would ever suspect him. Would dare suspect that it was a middle-age suitor that had been jilted for another man? Gerald's heart pounded with fear and trepidation.

Gerald justified the crime of passion to himself. "How could she choose him over me? Wasn't I the one who could entice Ophelia by providing love, desire, jewelry, and riches? How could she choose him over me? A man that had Valentino eyes, dark luxurious long hair, and a profile of Adonis? I could have given her a comfortable and stable life!
More justification came as Gerald walked stronger, faster, and recklessly down the alley way to his appointment. Gerald talked to himself in a harsh tone and said, "Maybe it would be boring living with me. The man of her dreams could have provided her all that her heart desired." Then Gerald came to a conclusion. "I could make up for what she was lacking or needing with money. Why, I could give Ophelia anything she wanted! Or anything she might have wanted. But it wasn't enough so I made a decision for both of us."

Two police cars drove swiftly towards the alley, flashing their lights and sounding their sirens. The sound of the sirens were so loud that Gerald had to cover his ears in torment. What was louder? The sound of the siren, the loudspeaker forcing him to give himself up, or the rapid beating of his own heart? The killer came out of the alley pale, shaking with hands up in defeat. Trying to catch his breath as the guilt and shame overtook him.

"He had been Ophelia's assailant!" Officer Kelly pointed his gun towards Gerald and said, "You are under arrest. Anything you say will be used in a court of law and can be used against you."

Gerald pleaded with the officer, "Sir, you must understand. If she had not chosen him everything would be perfect. We would be together right now." Gerald could see the mist that formed the frame of Ophelia staring at him. Ophelia was now a ghost, haunting him, and accusing him of her demise. Gerald whispered, "Oh my darling, if only you would have said, "Yes," before the final bullet was drawn."

The Sound of Quiet Voices

It seemed like a normal neighborhood. The cars passed by on their normal route to work. Children were getting on the school bus. People jogged or walked their dogs on the sidewalk. Another busy day for Wanda as she got ready for work. She looked out the window. She noticed that the neighborhood looked the same but the people were different. No one in the neighborhood really knew each other. They didn't talk or even say hello. They were lost in their own worries and concerns. They would walk in unconscious thought, looking at their phones or ipads.

She got in her car and went to work. When she got to work, she would try to talk to others. However, they were caught up in their lives. They were not able to listen or understand. She would sit with others and hear about what they had wanted to do. She would hear about what they could have done. Then, she would hear the discontent in their lives. There was no joy or hope in their words, only despair. She would try to mention about herself. However, they were not able to see beyond their own helplessness and longing.

She went for a walk. She noticed the people that were caught up in their machines, phones, and other electronic devices. No one really talked to each other. They were just there in the same space. She started noticing how quiet people were. They were talking by texting. No one spoke out loud. Wanda started thinking of an old song that summed up what she observed and how she felt. She was sad to see how her little town had changed. How the modern world had made a town, where there was a community spirit, to be one of just individuals. She hung her head and looked at the sidewalk. She realized the old song was made for the present age.

"And in the naked light I saw ten thousand people maybe more. People talking without speaking. People hearing without listening. People writing songs that voices never shared. No one dared disturb the sounds of silence. And the people bowed and prayed to the neon god they made. And the sign flashed out its warning. In the words that it was forming. And the sign said the "Words of the prophets are written on the subway walls, and tenement halls. Whispered in the sounds of silence."

—

Haunting Refrain

By Kathy Lou

A guitar played a sweet, haunting melody. People turned around to find out where it was coming from. It was coming from a book store around the corner. The owner of the shop had gone outside to practice.

People stopped to watch, and a crowd formed around the shop owner. The melody an old 1950s tune, but most people did not recognize the song. However, an old man in the crowd remembered it from his younger years. He started singing along with the melody.

The shop owner asked him to come up front and sing with him. He walked towards the shop owner, hunched over with a cane. He walked slowly towards the front of the store until he stood next to the shop owner.

The shop owner played the refrain to the song. The man started to sing …

"The autumn leaves drift by my window.
The autumn leaves of red and gold.
I see your lips, the summer kisses,
the sunburnt hands I used to hold."

The crowd stood in wonder and amazement. The blending of their sound was like nothing they had ever heard before. When the man finished singing, there was complete silence. Everyone wanted to capture the moment and keep it in their hearts. Then they clapped and cheered for both of them.

The shop owner put down his guitar and clapped for the man. The man smiled and bowed. The shop owner said he needed to open the shop back up. He asked the man if he would like to visit the shop and have a cup of tea with him.

The man said, "I would like that."

The crowd went their way, realizing that they had just witnessed two amazing and talented artists. The crowd continued on with their busy schedules. The shop owner and the man had a cup of tea and sang songs from the 1940s and 1950s.

Just for a moment, time stopped. The two men were singing the old songs and feeling young again. The old man did not have to focus on the pain that made him slump over and walk with a cane. The shop owner did not have to worry about business, record keeping, or the loneliness he felt. They were feeling young, 17 again, and happy.

They became good friends. People would stop and hear them sing and play. To think, it all started with a melody, a tune, and a magical moment.

The Man at the Diner

by Kathy (10/22/19)

Kate walked into the diner 30 minutes before closing time. She had worked a tiresome and exhausting shift at the factory and didn't want to cook. The waitress told her she could sit anywhere. Kate sat down and ordered a cup of tea. The waitress went back to the kitchen to boil some water.

A man at a nearby table watched as Kate sat down. He decided to introduce himself. "Hi! My name is Joshua. What's yours?"

Kate was shocked that a complete stranger talked to her in such familiar terms. "My name is Kate," she said suspiciously as the waitress brought her tea and took her order.

Joshua talked about being new in town. Kate spoke about the events in her town and a story she had read.

Joshua smiled and said, "I have been sent to tell you. God has heard your prayers."

Kate was curious. "How do you know my prayers?"

Joshua said, "Just believe. You will see things happen that you never expected." Joshua walked up to the counter, paid his tab, and left.

The next week, a new job posting came up in the want ads online. It was a job as a fashion designer. Kate had dreamed of being a designer since she was in high school. However, she worked 'hand to mouth' and had just enough money to pay her bills and care for her son. Being a single mom, and trying to make it alone, was tough.

She poured herself a cup of coffee, sat at the table, and glanced at the job description. Kate read the ad. *What have I got to lose?* she thought.

Kate filled out the application online. She received an email for an interview and set up the meeting for her day off. On the day of the interview, Kate wore the best skirt and blouse she could find. She brushed her hair and put on her make-up. She drove her son Kent to elementary school. Afterward, Kate drove to the job site and parked in the visitors' parking.

Kate nervously walked into Human Resources and introduced herself to the Human Resources manager. She was asked questions and given various scenarios in which she had to answer what she would do in a given situation. Kate had many life experiences where she had to make choices that required integrity, honor, and mutual respect at her job and in her neighborhood. Kate used these experiences to shape her answers. She thanked the manager and walked out the door.

Kate was flabbergasted when she received a call back that she got the job. The starting pay was more than she got in two months at the factory! Kate prayed and asked God if this was her answer to prayer. She felt encouraged that this was the answer she was seeking. Kate called Human Resources and accepted the position. Kate gave her two weeks' notice.

At the new job, Kate made new friends and moved to a better neighborhood and school district. She was able to learn skills and receive training for marketing the clothing line that she designed. Life was better and Kate worked a job doing what she had always wanted.

Suddenly, she remembered Joshua's words and realized that God heard prayers. Sometimes, when we are least aware, God puts angels among us when we need them the most. All we need is the faith of a mustard seed, and He can move mountains.

The Traveler

Jonathan noticed that the snow started falling and could see the soft flurries bring a bright and pure shade of white to the skies and the scenery around him. The snow started falling harder, and it became harder to see.

Jonathan realized that he would have to stop until the visibility was better on the roads. He noticed a restaurant with its lights on. He pulled off the road, drove into the parking lot, and parked the car. He walked inside and found an empty table.

The waitress came over and said, "What will you have?"

"I'll have a cup of coffee. I wonder when the snow is going to let up? I have a long way to go."

The restaurant was bustling because of the snow. Jonathan was glad that there was an open table. The waitress poured Jonathan a cup of coffee, and he felt that this would be another Christmas where he would be alone. His parents were getting older. His work and obligations prevented him from visiting them. He had finally taken a break and had some days off. *Why now are we having such a strong winter storm?* he thought.

The door jingled. A man walked in wearing a warm winter coat, hat, mittens, and winter boots. He asked the hostess for a table. Jonathan was annoyed but curious who the Christmas visitor was. He was annoyed because he looked like Santa Claus. He and Santa Claus had not been on good terms for a long time.

The waitress said, "We are all full. You will have to wait."

The man noticed Jonathan sitting by himself and asked if he could sit at Jonathan's table.

"Suit yourself. You can sit here. I'm just here till the storm calms down."

The traveler introduced himself and said, "My name is Kris. Where I am from, they call me Kris Kringle."

The waitress asked what Kris wanted to drink, and the visitor said, "Hot chocolate with extra whipped cream."

Madge, the waitress, brought him a steaming cup of hot chocolate, and Kris drank a sip. The whipped cream formed on his gray mustache.

"You have got to be kidding! Your name is like Santa Claus's," exclaimed Jonathan.

The old gentleman said, "You may not know me, but I know you. You are the little boy who wanted a sled that could outrace your brother down the hill."

Jonathan looked disgusted and said, "Yeah, I never got it. That was when I stopped believing. Wait a minute! How did you know that?"

"I'm sorry that you did not get your sled. The elves forgot to add it to my load for Christmas gifts." Kris Kringle looked at Jonathan and continued, "I have felt bad ever since, and I wanted to make it up to you."

Jonathan said, "Yeah, but I am 28 years old now, and I am not a boy! How can you make it up to me?"

Kris said encouragingly, "I know that you want to see your mom and dad and that they are praying for you. Therefore, I have brought my sleigh with my reindeer to get you there in record time. If I get you home and take you back to your car after Christmas, will you believe there is a Santa?"

Jonathan said, "If you do what you say, I will believe."

"Then, let's pay for our drinks and go!"

Jonathan was curious and wondered if the Christmas traveler was who he said he was. Outside the restaurant were a sleigh and reindeer. Surprisingly, the reindeer looked like Rudolph.

Jonathan got on the sleigh, and it magically traveled to his little town of Maine. Jonathan could not believe that he was home and had not missed the holidays.

When Jonathan got up the next day, a wrapped gift was under the tree. He noticed that box was big and contained something heavy and sturdy in it. He tore the wrapping off excitedly and opened the box. It was a Christmas sled that was meant for racing down the hill! It was motorized and was the top of the line.

There was a card attached. It said, "All you have to do is believe. Never forget to see Christmas through the eyes of a child, so you don't miss the Christmas magic."

Jonathan's eyes glistened, and he felt blessed and loved. Mom started playing songs on the piano, and Jonathan joined in on the songs. "Love and joy come to you and a cup of cider too. And God bless you and give you a Happy New Year. And God give you a Happy New Year!"

Pillow talk

By Kathy Lou

Anna Maria would talk in her sleep. Sometimes she would talk so loudly she could be heard in another room. When Anna woke up, she would never remember her dreams. She did not believe that she talked in her sleep.

"But you talk to yourself every night. It is keeping me Awake," Anna's roommate said.

Her roommate mentioned getting an appointment with a doctor.

Anna made an appointment and went to see the doctor. He decided to have her do a sleep study.

She lay on a bed where she could be monitored, with electrodes taped to her head and heart Anna turned the lights off and started dreaming.

The doctor watched the monitor. The monitor needle started rushing over the page. Then it made strange up and down patterns. Anna began to talk in her sleep, and her heart started racing. She jabbered, seeming upset. Anna called for help. Then she went back to sleep.

She dozed off and started dreaming again. This time she started talking like she was trapped and could not get out. She woke herself up. Anna realized that it was just a dream and went back to sleep.

When she woke up, the doctor gave her a report about the sleep study. He asked her about the restless nights she had been having. He asked about her eating habits, activity level, and stress in her life. She told him how hectic her life was. She mentioned the stress and that she did not get much sleep.

He told her about the things she was saying in her sleep. Anna had not realized that she had been talking all night. She remembered her dream. It was a dream about an experience from her childhood. She had forgotten this experience and how scared she was. However, she played out the scene in her dreams at night.

She talked to a counselor about her childhood experiences and had a good cry. When she came to terms with her fears and anxieties, she could sleep better at night.

She still thinks of her childhood and remembers the experiences from the past. However, she can now remember the good as well as the bad.

The Mist on the Water

It is a still, quiet night. No sounds of ducks or other wildlife. There is a chilling quiet. I walk through the woods, and all I hear is the sound of my own footsteps. I look around to see if anything is behind or in front of me. I hear nothing. There are no sounds – nothing but the beating of my own heart.

Suddenly, a mist rises from the water. It evolves and winds through the air, enveloping the trees, the grounds, and the surrounding forest. I think, *Where did it come from? What will happen next?*

All I see is the rising of the mist. I see the rain misting around me. The mist rises up into a deep, gray fog. I can't see in front of me. I am stuck, trying to find my way in the mist.

I am afraid but walk courageously. I need to stay strong even if I don't know if I can continue. I walk cautiously. I run to find a place to hide till the fog dissipates. My mind races. *Is this just an illusion or reality? Am I dreaming? Am I going through a valley of fear? Will I wake up in a cold sweat, and thank God this is not real?*

I can feel the cold, and my feet get soaked from the constant mist. I will believe that I will survive and walk forward. Although, I still don't know what I will stumble into. I must believe. I cannot tremble with fear.

Suddenly, I hear a voice. It gets closer and closer. It is the sound of someone I love that I have missed for a long time. It was a voice to remind me of gentler, younger days, when life was less complex. It was a time before bills, hardships, and struggles became the mainstays of my life.

I feel a warm touch on my shoulder. It is the one that I have longed to see. "But, this person is dead," I tell myself. "They are in heaven with God. How can I feel that this person is here?"

The fog lifts, and all I see is light. I am in a new place. I see many people that have died and gone on to the other side. We embrace, and I cry softly. What a joy it is to see them!

Then it occurs to me. I left the previous world when I was left alone in the mist.

The Muck and the Mire Part I

I used to go to the park to clear my head after a long day. I would walk, wondering how I would pay my bills, worried about my kids, life, and future. Even though I claimed I had faith, I still did not feel at peace. I walked through the park. It reflected the scenario in my heart and soul.

Near the bridge was a creek with a narrow path and trees surrounding both sides. Time and lack of care had caused the creek to be polluted and muddy. All you could see was the muck and the mire.

A place of natural beauty left to those who did not appreciate the wonder of what God had done. A habitat that should have been a place to support the ecosystem was a place of chaos. The water moved slowly, and I couldn't see any fish. It was a place that you walked through quickly. It did not look safe or a place to dwell and reflect. I got to thinking that is what a lack of peace is like. What was meant to be beautiful is forgotten. All that is left is turmoil and sadness. It was just another day like any other. I walked away the same as I walked in. Closing myself in from all around me.

The Muck and the Mire Part II

It was spring when I walked back to the lake. As I stood near the bridge, I noticed a sight that God had made. The water was flowing quicker than the last time I visited this site. Then I realized that it was a sight for me to see what He was doing in the stream and in me.

The muck and the mire were in the middle of the stream. The water was moving it away. The same pollution was still there.

The difference was that there was enough strength in the middle of the stream for the muck and mire to go away. God revealed how, like a cleansing stream, He removes what separates us from His presence.

God replaces it with peace and harmony. Amid the chaos, there is a peace that only comes from the hand of God.

I learned that I could not appreciate peace until I learned how God works in the middle of the chaos in my life.

I walked away, happy for the inner strength I was learning to have despite what was happening around me.

The Muck and the Mire Part III

The next time I went to the park was in summer. On my walk, God and I had a talk. He showed me what He was doing in my life. I discovered how He had been helping me to grow closer to Him.

He showed me a peaceful mountain stream. The stream that had moved slowly was clear, calm, and serene. The water reflected nature's art of trees, mountains, and animals. The water also reflected purity, and I sensed His presence in the mountain air. I thought of my first journey along this stream. I remembered the muck and the mire, leaves, pollution – everything that affected its constitution.

Now, everything was in natural order, and the park became beautiful and serene to me. God had done a wonder. It was plain to see. A wonder to the stream and to me.

I don't know how God revealed His plan. As He was doing this miracle, I didn't understand. He was clearing up things I did not want to see. He was bringing out the beauty in the stream and in me.

God's peace is a wondrous thing to see. I began to realize the love God had for me. Through this garden, He would walk hand in hand with me.

The way He works is a mystery. He works from day to day. Teaching us to follow Him in all we do and say. God does not tell us, as He works, what His total plan is. He knows that teaching, bit by bit, is easier to understand.

The Form on the Sand

By Kathy Lou

It was a balmy September evening, and I decided to go to the beach and take a late walk. I took off my sandals and felt the wet sand between my toes. Close to the bridge, I saw a strange object or figure I had not encountered before.

A form of a man sat on the wet, sandy beach as the dark grey clouds rolled past. The figure had a head, neck, and protruding spine. I looked closer to see if it was a creature that had died in its present state. The creature's leg was bent, and the thin boney foot was resting on the beach with toes outstretched. I assumed that whatever it was, was motionless and shallow without the ability to move.

The beach beckoned me on, and I walked past the form to discover what it was. The male figure had an amphibious quality like a frog. The sunken face of the creature looked out towards the sea. I realized that the form was not real at all. At least it was not real when I walked past it. The man was a motionless statue of driftwood.

I wondered what had happened to the man. He sat there long enough to conform to the sea and the beach. Then I understood that he was waiting for something to happen, such as peace, less self-absorbed friends, politicians that were actually 'for the people,' or love and harmony. World peace would be a nice thing to wait for.

I realized that the man was like me. I have waited for things to get better in my lifetime. I hoped for closer friends, family, connections, financial security, and a career that would shine in my field of endeavor.

None of these things happened. I cried and cried and realized that all you have in this life is life and death. People can be cruel, heartless, and self-centered. The only option you have is to be tough and hard and build an exterior of driftwood. Words and actions flow through you but don't have any substance to stay.

I wanted to sit with the figure. Suddenly I realized the closer I got to the mysterious figure, the dryer my skin became. The blood, tears, and substance left me, and I was in another state of consciousness. The wooden figure had changed me – I was a part of him and he had become a part of me.

I realized that my heart was becoming shallow like driftwood. I never wanted to love again. I would not let another human being hurt me or damage my spirit.

I walked off the beach as human driftwood and followed a shallow path just like the others before me. At this point, no one mattered. Politics, opinions, other humans, or what had hurt me before. All that mattered was the sand and the sea.

I had trouble getting into my car with my key. Finally, I opened the car door and sat in the driver's seat.

To my horror, I became motionless as the form I saw on the beach …

Beauty from Ashes

by Kathy Lou

Fire burns.
Red, orange, yellow
embers rise up
destroying everything
in its path.
Everything that you thought
you had was only temporary.
One hope remains
when the fire burns,
and you stand in the
midst of the burning coals,
you will find
beauty from ashes
hope from despair
a chance to be refined.
A chance to be strong again.

.

You can
find a path that's new.
A new beginning.
Beauty from ashes.
A chance to start again.

Troubled Mind

Goodbye to the dream
that I left behind.
It's time to go forward
to ease my troubled mind.

I thought it was forever –
a Cinderella dream.
Everything looks better
from the outside it seems.
Love goes good and bad,
no victims left behind.
We all have our own way
to ease our troubled mind.

Candle in The Dark

by Kathy Gilman (written 12/29/19)

(Verse 1)
When I am weak,
then You are strong.
My life, my God,
and my heart's song.
When hope seems dim,
and I feel defeat,
down on my knees
Your face I seek.

(Chorus)

You are my candle in the dark.
A rising sun,
a loving heart.
A love so strong,
just for me.
The love you showed on Calvary.
(Verse 2)
The world can be a scary place
with hate and war,
not a friendly face.
If the world could see
that we are one,
you could light a candle
for everyone.
(Back to chorus)

Songs from Toxic Love

Till the Final Goodbye (Ricardo's Theme)
(Soft guitar strum)
1. Dearest sweetheart, I love you, yes, I do. You know
I'll always care for you. But I must go. I'm sure you know.
Please don't cry. Just one more kiss, and then the final goodbye.
(Chorus)
I knew when we met, I would never regret, one
sunrise, one sunrise with you. But my journey takes a
path, that is known to very few. So I must bid you adieu.
2. Till that moment, think of a day. When we'll marry and I'll take you
away.
Until then, let us dance. I'll hold you tight. Just one more kiss,
then the final goodnight.
(Go to chorus)

A Summer Song (Katie's Song)
1. I dream of you and what we knew of summer's warm
embrace. Of what we lost and the high cost and what a
sad, sad waste. So many things left unresolved. So
many words unsaid. We finally drifted far apart from
the day when we first wed.
2. Now you have yours and I have mine. I've found a
love that's true. He treats me better than any man I
ever knew. I long to love and trust again. To feel both
young and new. To sing again a summer song better
than I had with you.
(Refrain)
I long to love and trust again. To feel both young and
new. To sing again a summer song better than I had
with you.

The Lover's Cry (Marta's theme)
(Calypso beat with guitar, conga drum and maracas)
(CHORUS)
Ohhhh how I long for his love. Oh oh .... How I long for
his touch. Oh ... how I long to be wrapped, with his
arms around me.
(same chords throughout the verses)

1. He leads a double life, but I'm still his wife. He says it's for me. He
fights for liberty. I sit all alone and wait by the phone. I pray he'll come
safely home to me.
(CHORUS)
2. I may never know the path he goes.
I trust it's for me, to protect our family. As he flies away,
I say "Just one more day. Let him come safely home to me."
(CHORUS)

The Broken Road

by Kathy Lou (5/4/22)

When the road you walk is broken
and you're feeling all undone.
When the new 'normal' is hard to deal with,
it's got you on the run.
Lord knows, you've still got to pay your bills
working as hard as you can.
Tough to be in this life
if you're not a Godly woman or man.

The Ghost From Vaudeville

By Kathy Lou

Joe Walker and Charlie Davis were finishing up their duties before the play started. Joe turned to Charlie with a worried look on his face. "I don't like being here on Halloween night," he said. "I keep hearing sounds near the stage door."

"What kind of sounds?" asked Charlie.

"It sounds like a man tap dancing. Sometimes there's singing, too. When I check, there is nobody there."

"Tap dancing? Singing? You must be imagining things," Joe scoffed.

"Yeah, it's the strangest thing. I don't see anybody, but I hear these sounds. I think the theater is haunted."

"Well, I don't believe in ghosts."

"Something strange is afoot! Alright, then you stay here after the show, around midnight. Tell me what you hear."

"OK, I will prove to you you are hearing things."

So, the two men stayed through the show, the curtain call, and watched the audience file out. They stayed late to clean up the theatre.

At the stroke of midnight, they heard the tap dancing. Suddenly, down on the stage, Joe and Charlie could see a man dressed in an old-style tuxedo. He was doing a slow tap dance routine and singing an old song from the 1920s. Spellbound, the two men watched him singing and dancing on stage. They looked at each other in amazement.

Charlie thought it was an optical illusion. The dancing man looked as real as either of them. Charley was used to seeing performers on that stage. The two janitors walked up to the man on stage.

The dancer proceeded to introduce himself. "Murphy Monroe's the name, best tap dancer this side of Missouri," he said.

He then resumed dancing. The dancer seemed real … but not real. There was a fuzzy quality about him, like he was always out of focus. That's when Charlie realized this was a ghost. The two men raced for the door.

The next night Charlie and Joe asked the stage manager if anything unusual had ever happened in the theater. The stage manager thought a moment and then answered, "Yes, it was something awful. Legend has it that in the 20s, a vaudeville performer was doing his act on this stage. Midway through his routine, a heavy burlap bag filled with sand fell on him from the rafters and killed him. Word was he was killed by a jealous suitor of Miss Josephine Booth, who was a leading lady in the show."

"What was the dead man's name?" asked Joe.

"I believe his name was Murphy Monroe," answered the stage manager.

Joe and Charlie couldn't believe it! Charlie and Joe started studying time travel and what it would take to build a time machine. They studied and compared notes. During their spare time, both gentleman took on the task of creating the device. When it was finally ready, they brought the machine to the prop room and put a cover over it. The machine was ready to go.

Legend has it, in the theater's prop room, the original plans described by HG Wells were drawn. What few people knew was it actually worked.

One evening, Charlie and Joe went into the prop room, got in the time machine, and set the gears for that fateful night. In their notes, it was calculated that they would need to be at the playhouse on June 21st, 1920, at 8:15 pm. Charlie and Joe buckled up their seat belts and flew through time and space to that night of our dancer's demise.

Charlie found Murphy Monroe backstage and warned him not to do his act. Monroe refused to believe him.

Since Monroe wouldn't budge, Charlie decided to stop the killer instead. He climbed up into the scaffolding and spied a man in a black cloak cutting the rope and holding up a large sand bag. When Charlie yelled, "Stop!" the other man dropped his knife and ran towards him.

They went at each other, but Charlie was larger and stronger and could beat the man unconscious. Once the man was in police custody, Charlie returned to the time machine and sent himself back to the present.

The next night, Charlie asked the stage manager about the ghost they'd seen.

Sam, the manager, said, "What ghost?"

"The ghost of Murphy Monroe."

"He's old, but he is not a ghost," laughed Joe. "He's been married to Josephine Booth, you know. Got seven children, grandchildren, and great-grandchildren."

Just then, an elderly grey-haired man shuffled from backstage and, with a big smile, paused to do a couple soft-shoe steps. Despite the man's advanced age, Charlie instantly recognized Murphy Monroe.

"I have wanted to thank you," exclaimed Monroe, "for saving my life!"

Charlie laughed. What do you know? A happy ending. The guy got the girl!

The Scapegoat

by Kathy Lou (Written 4/30/19)

Once there was a goat named Harvey. He was born into a large goat family. He was not treated any different than any other of his goat brothers and sisters. Sometimes he felt left out because his older brothers and sisters were doing the normal 'goat thing' for teenage goats. You know, 'goating each other on.'
Harvey was the middle goat in the herd. The younger goats were always 'miking' for attention. Sometimes Harvey would be forgotten out in the pasture, and one of the older goats would have to remind Mom and Dad Goat that Harvey was missing.

Well, Harvey got more depressed than defiant. "What if I ran away? They would not even miss me!" he muttered.

Harvey was determined to run away and see if he would be missed. He decided that he would run away in the middle of the night. While all the goats were sleeping, Harvey packed all his goat things in a suitcase and snuck out. Mom and Dad Goat were sound sleepers, so they did not hear the barn door open and close as he hit Harvey in the posterior on the way out.

The next morning, Mom Goat (Nannie) got up and started making breakfast for Dad Goat (Billy) and the other goats.

Nannie counted the chairs at the table and noticed that one of the goats was missing. But Nannie had so many goats and had lost part of her memory that she could not remember what goat was missing!

"Billy, can you figure it out?" she asked.

Billy was older than 50 in goat years and did not have much memory either.

Finally, one of the baby goats spoke up. She could not talk in full sentences, so this is what all the goats heard. "It's Harvey! He's a scape goat! Harvey scaped!"

She was trying to say Harvey ran away or escaped. Nannie and Billy searched for the scapegoat. The brothers and sisters gathered together and thought about their poor brother, Harvey.

The oldest brother Bobby Goat said, "I have a great idea! How about every time something gets lost or broken we blame the scapegoat? Mom and Dad will think it's Harvey!"

The brothers and sisters formed a pack and decided everything would be the scapegoat's fault. They would never get in trouble again if there was someone to blame.

Eventually, Harvey came back. However, the idea of the scapegoat continued, and Harvey was officially named the scapegoat!

Harvey realized that he should never have left because it did not improve his situation better. It only made it worse.

Through the years, the scapegoat idea was used whenever someone else did not want to take the blame. It was also used when others did not want to fix the problem. They just wanted to 'shed light' that things were not right. It must be someone's fault.

Harvey went on his way and was not seen again in the pasture. Every now and then, people think they see a lone goat. People just started saying, "Oh, that's Harvey. He can't be seen, just heard. Why he was the Harvey that might have inspired the rabbit story!"

By the way, if you see Harvey, tell him Nannie and Billy Goat are still looking for him.

The Two Packages

by Kathy Lou

Lucy drove home after an exhausting day at work. She immediately went to her room and decided to change into her favorite tee-shirt and sweatpants. She looked in the refrigerator, wondering what a healthy and balanced meal would be to cook for dinner.

The doorbell rang. At first, Lucy ignored it. Then it rang twice, and there was a knock on the door. Lucy looked out her door and saw a brown truck and a man in a brown shirt and pants at her front door.

Curious, Lucy went to the door. "Lady, here are two packages that you needed to sign for," said the UPS driver.

Lucy looked for the address where they were from, but there was no forwarding address. Lucy wondered if she should sign for and accept the packages.

Lucy always liked a good mystery, so she signed for the delivery and received the packages. One seemed rather heavy but the other was remarkably light. She put the packages on the front table.

Who would have sent them? I am not expecting anything. Will I like what is in the packages? What would I be expected to pay? she wondered.

Lucy's curiosity took her in all directions. She proceeded to make dinner but could not keep her mind off the packages in the front room. "I will open them after dinner. Who knows? It might be worth the wait!" she said to herself.

That evening she noticed that the first package seemed bigger and heavier and formed the shape of a box. The other package formed into a box, but it was still light when Lucy picked it up. The first box was hard to lift and seemed like it contained rocks. Lucy tried to take it outside, but the burden became too heavy. The large box opened, full of worries, troubles, everything that was hard to imagine and live with.

Lucy did not know why she accepted such a box. *Who could have brought such misery and despair to my home? How can I return it to its sender?* she thought.

Suddenly, Lucy came up with an idea. *Maybe the second box can help me with the first one,* she thought.

Lucy carefully opened the second box, and light sprang out. The light was brighter than anything she had ever seen. The light was so bright that it overpowered the first box, and lightning struck the heavy box of cares and woes. The heavy box closed itself and became just a package again.

The light continued to shine. Lucy got some masking tape and closed the first box. She wrote with a black felt pen, 'Return to Sender.'

Lucy finally understood the scripture about the importance of light. It can reveal what is hidden. It can bring truth where there is none. She also understood that burdens can get heavier when they are carried alone. When the light of God shines, and he is asked to guide you, the burden becomes light. We have the choice to accept or reject light but light will always shine through the darkness.

When a stick helped teach a lesson

(It's not what you think; believe it or not, it really happened.)

By Kathy Lou

A group of students that gathered in their usual meeting place. They said to each other, "You know, this place is too small for us. I got an idea! How about we meet at the river? We can get something to build with and build a place for all of us to meet!"

The teacher said, "OK, that's fine!"

One of the students gave it some thought and said to the teacher, "Why don't you come with us?"

The teacher said, "Why not? I'll join you."

They all went to the Jordan River. Since there were no chairs or a building, the students got industrious and started cutting down trees for their new classroom. As one of the students cut down a tree, his iron ax head fell into the water.

The student panicked and said, "Oh no! What am I going to do? I borrowed that ax for just this occasion."

The teacher observed the whole thing and asked, "Where did it fall?"

The student was frantic and showed him where he heard the first kerplunk of the ax head as it fell into the water.

This is where the stick (remember the stick that would have been overlooked?) came into the picture. The stick thought it would be an ordinary day but stuck around anyway. The teacher cut off the stick from its tree and threw it in the water where the ax head had sunk. The stick figured it would just sink and wondered what it was doing being thrown in the water.

Then a miracle happened! The ax head started floating upward just where the stick had been thrown! (I have heard of a coke float but never an ax head float.)

The teacher said, "Lift it out!" to the surprised student.

The student lifted the ax head out of the water.

This lesson spoke to me. I am only a 'stick,' and insignificant or unimportant. Things may not be perfect in my life, and I wonder if it will ever get better. This story teaches me that sometimes I have to return to the place where I gave up and put everything back in God's hands once again. He can work things out for good even when I can't see how it will ever be possible.

The teacher did not need a big building, fancy chairs, or a change of scenery. He and the students needed a big God who heard their cries and prayers. The same God that lifted the ax head with a stick also hears your prayers. Ask as you shall receive ... seek and you shall find ... knock and the door shall be open.

(The story is from 2 Kings 6:1–6 and the teacher's name was Elisha.)

When The Bottom Drops Out

When the bottom drops out
and you're barely breathing,
you don't think you will survive.
Thank God for the ones that you love
and the friends who are by your side.
You'll be glad that you're alive.
Sometimes you've got to go fishing,
sit by a cool mountain stream.
Take time to look up at the stars.
Things aren't as bad as they seem.
No, things aren't as bad as they seem.
When the bottom drops out
and you're barely breathing,
you don't think you will survive.
Thank God for the ones that you love
and the friends who are by your side.
You'll be glad that you're alive.
You'll be glad that you're alive.

Author memo: *The Lady in the Lake*

Congratulations on a great book of short stories! I felt this particular one, *The Lady in the Lake*, needed some work mainly to refine the timeline.

Timeline

Henry finding the 'body' was an excellent scene, and ditto the hospital and the visit of the police officers. However, the next scene with Martina and Felix kind of 'jumps the gun.' You will see that I interrupt it after saying "He had this charisma, chemistry, and energy. Martina was drawn to him like a magnet."

Then we start the story of how they met. Their meeting at the French restaurant confused me a bit, because it seemed initially as if there are only one (in the daytime), and then, a bit further on, there is a meeting in the evening (when they dance), and a further one where Felix is waiting for Martina outside the gallery. But on all these occasions it seemed as if they were meeting for the first time. I've tried to separate it into subsequent meetings, so that you start off with a meeting in the afternoon, then moving to the one in the evening (where he initially scares her), then moving to other meetings where they dance. I've changed the evening meeting to a Monday, because this would explain why Martina was so surprised at Felix. This builds tension because each time Martina feels something is off with this guy, but she ignores her intuition.

Martina ignoring her intuition is vital in this story, because one would wonder why is she sticking with this guy? The sentence of yours about Martina being like a fly in a spider web was excellent. She was stuck because he trapped her.

The scene with Felix and the voice in the kitchen is sooooo good! I moved some of the police scenes (e.g. where George Adamo comes to give information, and where they go to the computer room) and where they visit Rachel's mother to follow in short sequence, to build more tension.

Here I discovered an anomaly in the plot (the only one). In the computer room, they said Rachel was discovered at the bottom of the stairs, but Rachel's mom said she fell from a cliff when they were walking in the mountains. I stuck to the 'bottom of the stairs' story. So, I created a reason for why we should be suspicious of Felix – enter the neighbors who heard shouting on that day, and also said they heard them fighting frequently. Also, I deleted the bit that said they were married for 20 years.

I did some tidying at the end, with Felix seeing himself on the TV, finding out Martina is not dead, and being arrested.

Loved the ending, with all the ends neatly (and very fairly) tied together. Especially Felix's sentence in that old prison is delightful. And Martina and George!! Great story altogether.

General editing

Generally, your writing is crisp and visual (which is why I mention 'scenes,' as in a movie). You can add to this by using 'train of thought,' where you capture the character's thoughts as if in dialogue. However, we don't use quotation marks to indicate this dialogue, we use italics. The rules of punctuating a dialogue apply.

Of course, these are all suggestions. After all, you are the author!

Once again, congratulations!

Izelle Theunissen (editor)

Acknowledgments

The Sounds of Silence

"The Sound of Silence", originally "The Sounds of Silence", is a song by the American music duo Simon & Garfunkel. The song was written by Paul Simon over several months in 1963 and 1964. The duo's studio audition of the song led to a record deal with Columbia Records, and the original acoustic version was recorded in March 1964 at Columbia Studios in New York City for their debut album, Wednesday Morning, 3 A.M. Released on October 19, 1964.

https://en.wikipedia.org/wiki/The_Sound_of_Silence

The Autumn Leaves

"Autumn Leaves," composed by Joseph Kosma and featuring lyrics by the French poet, Jacques Prevert, debuted as "Les Feuilles Mortes." Yves Montand performed the song in the 1946 poetic realism film, *Les Portes de la Nuit*, a dark drama set in post-World War II Paris.

Johnny Mercer penned English lyrics for the tune in 1949, re-releasing it under the name "Autumn Leaves." Jo Stafford was the first to record the English version, but the song did not gain popularity until 1955, when pianist Roger Williams recorded a version of the song. The Williams rendition became a number-one hit, selling over one million copies.

The lyrics of "Autumn Leaves" pair with the gloomy feel of *Les Portes de la Nuit*, depicting the loss of a loved one and fading memories as time passes. The narrator laments, "Since you went away the days grow long/ And soon I'll hear old winter's song/ But I miss you most of all my darling/ When autumn leaves start to fall."

Following Williams' recording, artists including Steve Allen, Mitch Miller, the Ray Charles Singers, Jackie Gleason, and Victor Young recorded renditions of "Autumn Leaves," helping establish the song as a jazz standard.

"Autumn Leaves" remains a popular choice for novice jazz players, as the chord progression remains within the circle of fifths. Voice leading is relatively standard, though just before the end, chromatically descending chords may pose some challenges to performers.

https://performingsongwriter.com/autumn-leaves/